THE SKELETON WARRIOR

ADAM BLADE

ORCHARD

MEET TEAM HERO ...

JACK

POWER: Super-strength

LIKES: Ventura City FC

DISLIKES: Bullies

RUBY

POWER: Fire vision

LIKES: Comic books

DISLIKES: Small spaces

DANNY

POWER: Super-hearing

LIKES: Pizza

DISLIKES: Thunder

GENERAL GORE

POWER: Brilliant warrior

LIKES: Carnage

DISLIKES: Unfaithful minions

CONTENTS

MS STEEL reached for her mug of tea, but then paused as ripples spread across its surface. She could feel the tremors through her feet.

"Shockwaves, close by," said Professor Rufus, his fingers tapping at a keyboard. "It must be another portal opening."

Ms Steel glanced around the Team Hero Global Command Centre. The room was built into the bedrock beneath Hero Academy, and the pale sandstone flashed with the light of computer screens. Teachers hurried past, speaking in urgent voices. She looked past them to the maps lit up on the walls. Sure enough, a small light blinked on, just off the coast of Ventura City. It joined clusters of others dotted across countries and seas all around the world — each one a portal from Noxx.

Ms Steel steadied herself against a chair, struck with the full horror of what was happening. *Noxx is invading the surface. Just like it did a thousand years ago.*

"How many now?" asked a deep voice behind her. Ms Steel shook her purple hair from her eyes and turned to Chancellor Rex. The headmaster's face was wrinkled in a deep frown, and Ms Steel thought he looked older than ever.

"That makes ninety-six so far," said Ms Steel, grimly. *Ninety-six places where the Noxxian armies can enter our world and attack us ...*

A teacher with diamond-shaped scales on her face swivelled in her

chair. "The students have been armed and readied," she said.

Chancellor Rex nodded. "Thank you, Mrs Hindmarch."

A forked tongue flicked nervously across the woman's lips. "Can anything stand against this?" she

whispered to the headmaster.

"We must try," said Chancellor Rex firmly. "Have we heard from the rest of Team Hero?"

"The final outposts in Australia and China have reported back," said a teacher studying a computer screen.

A pair of white wings sprouted from her shoulder blades. "Every hero around the world is ready to fight, Chancellor."

"That is something, at least," said Rex. He walked over to the map of Europe, where two more portals had opened in Germany and the Swiss Alps. His hands closed into fists, blood draining from his knuckles. Ms Steel went over and touched his arm.

"Team Hero defeated General Gore before," she said. "We can defeat him again."

"Last time the heroes won because they found a weakness in Gore's armies," said Chancellor Rex.

Ms Steel nodded. Gore's forces had been destroyed by sunlight. They could only fight in darkness and shadow. But over the past few weeks Noxxian creatures had come through portals in broad daylight.

The Chancellor closed his eyes. "We must put our trust in the prophecy."

Ms Steel recited the words in her head: *Darkness will rise and conquer light, unless the Chosen One joins the fight.*

"While we have Jack Beacon on our side, there is still hope," she said.

A shout went up from across the

command centre. Several more portals
had opened up in Asia, and teachers
gathered around the map. The
Chancellor hurried over.

Ms Steel watched him go. She bit
her lip, holding back the doubts
worming themselves into her head.
*What if the invasion has come too
soon? What if Jack's not ready to face
Gore?*

Her jaw set in determination.
Whatever happened, she wouldn't
let Jack fight without all the help
he could get. *It's time. He must
have the weapon of light.* It would
mean travelling thousands of miles,

across the world, to the desert of her homeland.

But distance was no problem for Ms Steel.

She grabbed her laser lance from where it leaned against a desk, and stowed it in a harness on her back. Standing in the shadows at the back of the chamber, she conjured an image of her destination in her mind. Energy surged through her. For a second she was suspended in bright purple light. The air crackled.

When Chancellor Rex looked over, Ms Steel had vanished.

CHAPTER 1

THE PORTAL ORB

JACK CRAWLED on all fours through the darkness. He could hear Ruby scrambling along somewhere behind him.

"Let me get this straight," Ruby said, her voice echoing in the narrow metal tunnel. "General Gore's armies are about to invade."

"Yes," said Jack.

"Everyone else is forming into their units," Ruby went on.

"That's right," Jack said.

"So tell me," said Ruby, "why are we crawling through an air vent?"

"Just wait and see," Jack replied.

Ruby grumbled. They turned a corner, and lines of light entered the shaft through a steel grate. Jack crawled over and peered down through the slats. The room below was full of gleaming machinery, as well as crates of wires and tools.

"The technology lab?" Ruby hissed, peering beside him. "Why are we sneaking in here?"

"I heard Professor Rufus talking to Miss Gallagher," Jack whispered. "He's been building a portal creator. We'll need it to get into Noxx."

Ruby's face softened. Her orange eyes glistened with the same worry Jack felt when he thought of their friend trapped somewhere in Noxx. Danny had been infected by shadow and transformed into a terrifying bat creature. Despite this, he'd still saved Jack's parents from Gore's lizard servant Raptrix, dragging him through a portal back into Noxx.

"That's why we're here?" said Ruby

quietly. "You want to go to Noxx now?"

"We can't leave Danny there any longer," Jack said. "Besides, Chancellor Rex is busy organising the defences. We should go before he realises what we're up to."

When Jack first told the headmaster that he planned to go to Noxx to rescue Danny, Chancellor Rex had forbidden him. He'd said it was far too dangerous. Jack knew he was right — but how could he leave Danny trapped with their enemies?

Ruby's jaw set with determination. Jack knew she felt the same. "You're right," she said. "Let's do it."

After checking the coast was clear, Jack grabbed the metal slats. His hands glowed, flowing with his super-strength — the power that had earned him a place at Hero Academy. The grate was welded to the vent, but Jack tore it off with ease.

He jumped down into the lab, followed by Ruby. His red and silver bodysuit was covered in dust. He brushed it down, checking that the Shadow Sword still hung safely at his side. Jack was immune to shadow and the only human who could wield the Noxxian blade, which had once belonged to General Gore himself. With it Jack could close off portals, and he'd also used it to defeat three of Gore's own lieutenants. He was sure to need it in Noxx.

Ruby rubbed patches of grime from her yellow and silver bodysuit. On her back, she wore a mirrored shield Professor Rufus had designed to reflect and focus her flame vision. "What now?" she asked.

Jack began to inspect the gleaming machines around the lab. "The portal generator must be here," he said. He heard a beeping sound and looked over as Ruby jumped back from a tall robot with blaster arms.

"Do we know what it looks like?" she asked.

Jack shook his head. "Can you help us, Hawk?"

Instantly, the device hooked round his left ear vibrated and a visor slid out over his eye. Hawk was Jack's Oracle — an Oral Response and Combat Learning Escort. It was a computer, communicator and battle-tool all in one. Every Hero Academy student had one.

"Hello, Jack," Hawk said. *"I see we're in the technology laboratory. You're not ... replacing me, are you?"*

"Course not!" said Jack. "What would I do without you? We need to find something that can make a portal."

"Naturally! Just one moment."

Crosshairs appeared on the visor and Hawk began scanning each item of machinery in turn. Data flowed across the screen. *"Hologram projector,"* Hawk said. *"Laser drill, 3D printer, prototype cloaking device ... Wait a minute. I think this might be it."*

The crosshairs were fixed on a grey ball sitting beside a broken computer screen. Jack went over to it.

"That thing?" said Ruby. "It looks

like an old football."

On closer inspection, Jack saw that
its metal surface glowed softly. He
reached to pick it up.

*"I strongly recommend you don't
touch it!"* Hawk said in alarm. *"It's a*

Portal Orb. My analysis shows it's never been used before."

"It's our only chance to save Danny," Jack said. "We have to try ..." There was a small switch on the top. Jack pressed it and the orb hummed. Its surface swirled with dazzling colour.

"Wow," breathed Jack. He put his hand to it — and felt a powerful force pulse up his arm. "I think it'll work if you just touch it! Quickly!"

Ruby put her hand next to his. The humming grew louder. She raised her voice over the noise, "How will it know we want to go to Noxx?"

Immediately, the lab lurched from

under Jack's feet. There was a flash of light, and a falling sensation, like he was going down a roller coaster.

"I think it understood you!" Jack shouted, but his words were snatched away by a roaring wind.

Then there was nothing but darkness. Jack heard Ruby shouting something, but she seemed very far away. He fell down, down, down …

Lights trailed around him, like shooting stars. They dimmed and formed into a rocky landscape. Jack slowed, then jolted to a stop. He was lying on stony ground, Ruby beside him. Above them, jagged stalactites hung down from a high ceiling.

"You OK?" Ruby asked.

"Yeah." He sat up. They were on a ridge looking out across a gloomy cavern that stretched as far as he could see. The only light came from a

gigantic river of lava. It snaked past a
palace made of black stone, with tall
twisted towers.

Jack felt a shiver down his spine.
He turned to Ruby, heart racing.

"It worked," he said. "We're in Noxx!"

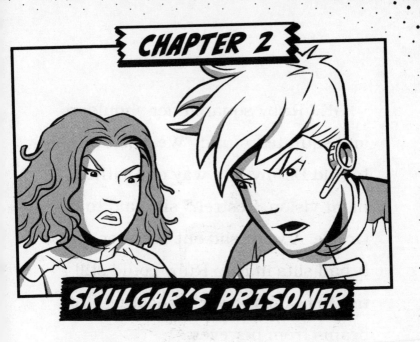

CHAPTER 2

SKULGAR'S PRISONER

RUBY WAS peering anxiously through the gloom. "We're in Noxx," she said, "but the Portal Orb isn't!"

Jack glanced around too. She was right. "The orb must only work one way," he said. "Well, we can't worry about that now. We'll just have to find another way back to the surface."

"OK." Ruby squared her shoulders and squinted round. "We won't be able to find Danny or a way out without night vision. Kestrel?" she said to her Oracle. A visor slid out over her eyes. It had slits in it so Ruby could still use her superpower — shooting fire-beams from her eyes.

Jack activated his own Oracle, visor flipping into place. *"Well, now look where we are,"* Hawk said. *"Activating night vision mode."*

Everything suddenly became washed in a greenish tinge — and crystal clear. Jack saw spired fortresses made of dark rock, and a crater in front of damaged stone buildings. *That must be blast damage from the bomb I dropped through the portal when I fought Chiptra.*

Beyond the crater was a sight that made Jack's blood turn to ice. Thousands of warriors were assembling across the rocky plains.

"Look, Ruby," he said. "Team Hero has no chance against an army so huge."

Instead of answering, Ruby suddenly dragged him behind a pillar. "Shhh!" she hushed him, pointing down to where the river of lava snaked close by. On its bank marched

a horde of armoured skeleton warriors, swords flashing dully in the dim red light.

"Let's just hope Chancellor Rex has a plan to deal with them," whispered Ruby. "And we need one too if we're going to save Danny. Any ideas?"

Jack was about to shake his head when he saw a flock of terrawings flap past, their vicious beaks open as they shrieked. He remembered how their cries had hurt Danny's super-sensitive ears — until he'd activated the sound defences on his Oracle ...

"That's it!" said Jack. "Hawk, can we tune in to Danny's Oracle?"

"Let me try. Scanning for Owl."

Jack held his breath as data scrolled down his visor.

"Owl located!" Hawk said.

Jack grinned as Hawk loaded a map of the cavern on the visor over his eye.

"The red dot shows where he is," said Hawk. *"I'll link up with Kestrel so Ruby can see, too."*

Jack traced the route from the red dot back to their position. "We have to go over the river, past the skeletons."

Ruby risked a glance down at the enemy. "I guess our stealth training in Ventura City should pay off."

"Too bad we don't have stealth

packs, though," Jack said. "Some camouflage would be nice."

"We'll just have to be quiet and quick," said Ruby.

They set off, scrambling down the ridge to the bank of the river. They ran from boulder to boulder, keeping low.

If we're seen, it's all over.

They paused at a stone bridge. The bones of the skeleton soldiers marching along gleamed in Jack's night vision. He noticed a huge figure, the size of a wrestler, with a bald head. He was waiting for the skeletons by a buzzing arch of metal that had wires trailing off it.

"Hurry up!" the large creature barked. "The invasion is almost starting! You need Darkcoat or the sun of the surface lands will turn you to ash!"

"Yes, Bulk," chorused the skeletons as they trooped forwards into the machine, ten at a time. A dark cloud sprayed them from jets on the insides of the arch, then seemed to seep into them and vanish.

"The Noxxian warriors we've fought in daylight must have had this Darkcoat on," Ruby whispered. "Otherwise they wouldn't have been able to go above ground."

Jack nodded. "This could be our chance to get past," he whispered, "while they're all facing the machine."

He ran at a crouch on to the bridge, Ruby just behind. Jack's heart thudded in his chest, and he knew that if any skeletons looked round they would be spotted. They reached the other side and scurried behind the ruined pillars of what looked like an old Noxxian temple, carved with a black sun.

"Made it," said Ruby, panting. "Where now?"

Jack checked the map. "This

way." He headed towards a platform suspended on wires, like a lift. "We've got to take this up there," said Jack, pointing up. High above, wide steel walkways ran between dark stalactites hanging from the cavern ceiling, as big as apartment blocks. Jack stepped on to the lift. There were only two buttons.

"Press the up button to go up," said Hawk. *"And the down button—"*

"Thanks, Hawk," Jack interrupted. He pressed the top button and felt his stomach lurch as they shot upwards. Beneath them he spotted hundreds of sleek black vehicles, like jet planes, standing in a wide crater. "What are those?" Jack wondered aloud.

"They look like space shuttles," Ruby said, looking puzzled.

"Hawk?" Jack asked.

"Portal Ships," Hawk replied, after a quick scan.

"I bet they're going to carry Gore's warriors to the surface," Jack said, panic rising in his chest. *There are enough ships to hold thousands of warriors. How will Team Hero beat them?*

The lift juddered to a halt just a few metres below the rocky ceiling. Jack and Ruby stepped out on to a steel walkway. It stretched towards a large black stalactite that was dotted with red windows.

"The map says Danny's in there somewhere," Jack said.

Ruby nodded, her expression determined. She hefted her mirror shield in front of her and Jack drew the Shadow Sword. Together, they advanced along the narrow walkway. Jack tried not to look down, but out of the corner of his eye he could see the skeleton soldiers massing like a thick horde of ants. *I hope they don't look up.*

The end of the walkway hugged the

side of the stalactite. As he reached it, Jack heard a cry of pain. He rushed to peer through a window — and gasped with horror.

A figure stood in a bare room that flickered with torchlight. He was shaped like a boy, but his skin was leathery and dark grey. Two great bat wings spread from his shoulder blades. His hands had shining claws. His eyes were completely black.

"Danny," Ruby whispered at Jack's side. Her voice was shaky.

Jack's fists clenched. "We're going to save him," he whispered. "There's got to be a way to change him back!"

Jack stepped towards the door but Ruby caught his arm. She nodded to the other end of the room, where a second figure strode into sight. Tall and broad, he was a skeleton, dressed in a horned helmet and a fur-lined cloak. His head was just a skull, with flashing red eyes. As the creature's cloak swished aside, Jack caught a glimpse of glass vials hanging from a belt. The skeleton pulled one out and tore away the stopper.

"Can you feel the power of the shadow?" the skeleton said. Jack's breath caught in his throat.

"Yes, Lord Skulgar," said Danny. His

friend's voice sounded croaky and dry
— but it was still Danny. Anger boiled
inside Jack.

What are they doing to him?

"Embrace the darkness," Skulgar
boomed, sweeping the vial around.

"Drive the light from your mind. Only then will you truly be a Noxxian."

From the vial came great clouds of velvety blackness.

Shadow!

The shadow swirled around Danny, who groaned as if in pain.

Jack could take it no longer. He jumped through the window, golden hands throbbing with power. Ruby landed by his side, holding the mirror shield.

Skulgar whirled around, eyes burning red. Danny looked up at them in surprise. For a second Jack wondered if he even recognised them.

"Attack!" Skulgar cried.

At the sound of the skeleton warrior's voice, Danny's confusion disappeared. He let out a scream so terrible it made Jack cover his ears, then grabbed a spiked club from a nearby rack.

With a beat of his wings, he leapt at Jack, swinging the weapon in a vicious arc. Jack froze, stunned by the speed of the attack, and not wanting to hurt his friend. He seemed to watch in slow motion as the club whirled through the air, straight at the side of his head.

CHAPTER 3

A FIGHT TO THE DEATH

THE GLINT of the club's spikes in the torchlight brought Jack to his senses. His training from Ms Steel's combat lessons kicked in, and he ducked. The wind from the swinging club ruffled his hair. He scrambled aside, but Danny was already coming at him again, throwing the club down in a brutal strike.

Clang!

It struck Ruby's shield. "Stop it, Danny!" she yelled, pushing him back.

Skulgar let out a low chuckle. "He is mine, now, heroes."

The skeleton warrior grabbed a long trident made of bones. Its three prongs looked needle-sharp. He jabbed it at Ruby. She met it with her shield. As the trident struck, it released a cloud of stinking black shadow. The back of Jack's throat stung and he fell to his knees, coughing. He sensed someone standing over him, and rolled, just ducking under Danny's club. Ruby had quickly crouched down to avoid the shadow — now she grabbed Jack and pulled him towards the window. They scrambled back through it and out on to the bridge. Jack gratefully sucked in the cleaner air.

Footsteps sounded behind them. Jack whirled round to see Danny striding over the bridge towards him and Ruby, Skulgar close behind.

He's using Danny as a shield, Jack thought angrily. *He knows we won't hurt our friend.*

Danny swung the club in front of him. Jack and Ruby backed away.

"Got a plan?" Ruby whispered to Jack.

"I think so. I'll get Danny out of the

way, then you blast Skulgar with a
fireball."

"OK, but how?" Ruby asked. "If you
get close, Danny's club will crush your
skull."

"Then I'll just have to get the club
away from him," Jack said. "Grab the
guard rail. Tight."

Ruby did as he asked. Bending down,
Jack gripped the walkway with his
glowing fists. Feeling the strength
surge through his fingers, he twisted
the walkway so it lurched to one side.
Metal shrieked and rivets popped.
Danny grabbed for the rail, dropping
the club over the side of the walkway

as he did so. In a flash, Jack ran down the walkway and crash-tackled his friend, pulling him to the floor.

"Now!" he cried, and looked back to see Ruby shoot a massive fireball right at Skulgar.

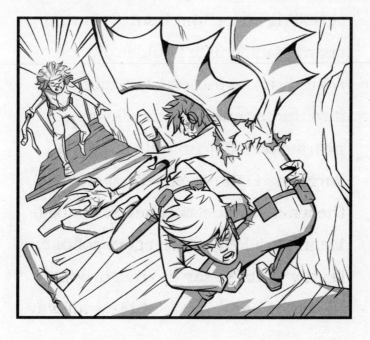

But Skulgar was quick too. He dropped to the floor and the fireball flew over him, hitting one of the stalactites.

BOOM!

A massive chunk of rock blew off it, revealing sharp and faintly glowing crystal inside. The boulder of rock soared through the air and smashed into the far end of the walkway, nearly tearing it from its supports. Jack and Danny were thrown over the side. Jack desperately scrambled for a handhold and his golden fingers clutched the walkway's edge. With his other hand, Jack grabbed hold of Danny's leathery arm. In one movement, he swung a stunned Danny back up and on to the walkway.

Still dangling from the bridge, Jack looked down. He groaned. The commotion had drawn the attention of hundreds of soldiers, who were staring up at him.

Now all of Noxx knows we're here ...

"Get back up, Jack!" cried Ruby from above, and he tugged himself up on to the damaged walkway.

Skulgar was advancing on Ruby, thrusting his trident. It sparked off the mirror shield as she blocked it.

Jack drew the Shadow Sword and charged, but again the skeleton warrior proved too quick. He spun and blocked Jack's blow with his trident. The Shadow Sword was caught between two prongs.

Skulgar leaned towards Jack. He could smell his dead, putrid breath. "The General will be disappointed," Skulgar rasped. "He was looking forward to killing the Chosen One himself. But now I have the pleasure of destroying you and ending the prophecy for ever."

"I don't think so," said Jack. With a grunt he shoved Skulgar back, freeing the Shadow Sword. The skeleton fell against the railing, his helmet rolling over the side.

Jack swung the sword.

Skulgar blocked with his trident but the force of Jack's strike broke the weapon in two. Jack's blade cleaved through Skulgar's body. Bone chips flew like shrapnel and one stung Jack's temple. Skulgar crumpled into a heap.

Jack heard a creaking sound, and realised he had cut clean through a main support beam holding the walkway together. With a splintering groan, the walkway fell away beneath

Jack's feet. His stomach dropped as he and Ruby plunged into thin air.

Someone was screaming, and he realised a moment later that it was him.

This is it. We're going to die in Noxx.

CHAPTER 4

FIGHTING THE ARMY

THE BREATH rushed from Jack's chest as something slammed into his side. A firm arm wrapped around his waist. He looked up to see ...

"Danny!"

Danny grinned, baring his long fangs. He held Ruby with his other arm. "I could get used to these bat wings," he croaked, soaring between stalactites. "Though I can't fly far with you two lumps."

Jack gaped at him in amazement. Was Danny cured? How had he fought off the shadow?

Before he could ask, they were swooping towards an empty patch of ground. Jack's body tensed as Danny's claws skidded against the dusty rock, but he and Ruby were both set down safely.

Danny picked up his club from where it was lying on the ground. He grinned. "I thought I could see it! Bat eyes are pretty useful too!"

"You saved us, Danny," Ruby said, raising her hand to slap him on the back. Her eyes widened. "Your wings are shrinking!"

Jack stared in wonder. Danny's wings were indeed shrivelling up into his shoulders. Danny was looking down at himself too.

"I'm changing back!" he said.

His voice had returned to normal. The claws on his hands were replaced by fingers. His rough, grey skin turned smooth and his fangs drew up into his gums. Hair sprouted on his head, and his eyes turned back to their old brown. After a minute, Jack and Ruby's friend stood before them.

Danny reached up and brushed his long, pointed ears with his fingertips. "Phew! Still there."

"What happened?" asked Ruby. "How did the shadow leave you?"

"It was weird," said Danny. "I can't really explain it. I saw you two falling, and something snapped inside me." He shook his head, as if he still couldn't believe it. "It was like having a light switched on inside my brain. I just knew I had to save you."

"It's good to have you back," Jack said. His smile faded as tremors tingled the soles of his feet. Ruby was staring past his shoulder.

"I think you need to see this."

Jack turned. Across the plains of Noxx, as far as the eye could see, Gore's armies were on the move. He could make out cockroach creatures armed with spears, lizard-men, like smaller versions of Raptrix, and huge beasts like mammoths with barbs all over their hides and four black tusks. Most were marching in squadrons towards the Darkcoat machine beneath the broken drawbridge.

Flocks of terrawings soared above, their screeches ear-piercing even from this distance away.

"Once they've all got their Darkcoat they'll board the Portal Ships," Jack said grimly. "The invasion has started."

"We have to stop them," Ruby cried. "But how?"

Danny whipped round. "I can hear something coming," he said. "There — skeletons! Heading this way!"

A troop of warriors was charging over the plains towards them. Their swords and spears glistened in the glow of the crystal stalactite Ruby had blown open. It gave Jack an idea. It might be their only chance.

"Most of the warriors haven't been through the Darkcoat machine yet," he said. "They're still vulnerable to light."

"What light?" Ruby asked. "Have you forgotten we're underground?"

Jack pointed up at the stalactites. "The crystal inside the rock! That's our source of light."

Ruby frowned, still not understanding.

Jack tapped his temples, by his eyes. "Remember what Ms Steel told us once. *Trust your powers.*"

"Of course!" Ruby cried. She bent

her knees, arching her neck to gaze towards the ceiling. She blinked, then took a breath.

Whoosh! Beams of fire shot from Ruby's eyes, lighting up the dark cavern like fireworks. They exploded

into the crystal in a brilliant dazzle of light, so bright that Hawk instantly switched off Jack's night vision.

The skeleton soldiers held up their hands, trying to block out the light. Some fell to the ground. The crystal stalactite shattered, huge glowing boulders raining down. The soldiers broke formation in a desperate bid to avoid them.

Whoosh! Ruby blasted the next stalactite apart too, then a third and a fourth. The Darkcoat machine was blasted into pieces by a shower of crystal boulders.

With a blood-chilling war cry, the

fleeing skeletons came charging towards them. Danny ran at the creatures, swinging his club in wild arcs. Jack held the Shadow Sword ready, but he knew he and Danny didn't stand a chance against so many warriors.

He glanced at Ruby, who was still firing at the ceiling. *We've got to speed this up*, he thought.

"Ruby, I need to use your mirror shield!" he shouted.

She frowned at him, eyes still glowing. Then she nodded in understanding and tossed the shield to him. Jack caught it, crouched down and angled it towards the ceiling.

"Light 'em up, Ruby!" Jack cried.

As Ruby fired, Jack tilted the
shield so the fire-beams reflected off
its smooth surface. The force made
the shield shake in his hands. Fire-
beams bounced off it in all directions,
shooting back up at the other
stalactites. The metal shield turned
hot, but Jack didn't let go. The cavern
roof erupted into a glittering display
of light.

Jack heard a wave of sound and
realised it was the cries of the
Noxxian army. The plains were
brighter than a desert and Jack had

to squint to make out the cockroach creatures, lizard soldiers and skeletons in the distance. He felt a surge of triumph. They were turning into ash, falling like dominoes as the light spread.

"It's working!" Danny cried, as the soldier he was fighting collapsed into a pile of dust. "Keep going, Ruby."

She grunted with the effort but kept up the bombardment. At last, the sound died away. Smoke hung over an empty landscape, filled only with discarded weapons and armour, shining in the light of the crystals.

The army is defeated!

"We did it!" said Jack, grinning at his friends. "We destroyed Noxx's army!"

The three friends bumped their fists together.

"There won't be an invasion now!" said Ruby, her eyes shining.

"I can't wait to tell everyone at school about this," said Danny. "Imagine Olly's face when he hears we've stopped Gore's army! How did you two get down here to Noxx, anyway?"

Jack and Ruby exchanged a glance. "Well ..." Jack began — but then he froze.

Out of the smoke was striding a

great shadowy figure. He was tall
and clad in black armour, his shadow
cloak rippling like liquid. He glared
down, only his flashing red eyes

visible within the
shadows of his
helmet.

"General Gore,"
Jack gasped.

Behind the
General came
the huge bald
man called Bulk.
A second figure
followed, smaller
and hunched,

with long, thin fingers and a smirk on his pale face. The General's red eyes burned with fury.

"Finally we meet, Chosen One," he hissed. "Each one of my lieutenants has failed to destroy you. So now it falls to me."

"Too late," Jack replied, his voice sounding calmer than he felt. "You have no army now."

The General roared in anger. With a quick movement he pulled a blaster from his belt and fired two rapid streams of shadow at Ruby and Danny. They both leapt aside just in time. Before Danny could recover,

Bulk grabbed him with one of his brawny arms.

As Ruby ran to help Danny, Gore fired a third stream of shadow, straight at Jack. He had no time to duck, but held out the Shadow Sword. The blast hit the blade with a powerful kick and Jack was flung backwards, the sword wrenched from his grip.

Jack hit the ground. The Shadow Sword arced through the air then came down point first, sticking into the ground. Jack scrambled to his feet and lunged towards it.

A bony grip tugged him back by

the shoulder. He looked up into
the smirking face of Gore's gaunt
henchman.

"Stop him, Smarm!" Bulk called.

Jack pulled free from Smarm and
scrambled towards the sword again.
But to his horror, General Gore bent
down and pulled the sword from the
ground before Jack could reach it.

"It is true that you have destroyed
my armies," Gore said. "But you have
delivered the Shadow Sword to me.
In my hands it is more powerful than
any army you can imagine. And the
first thing I will do with it is get rid of
the Chosen One, once and for all."

CHAPTER 5

THE DUEL

GORE BOOMED with laughter and
swung the sword around his head.
Jack didn't know what to do. He had
no weapon. He could suddenly feel
every bruise, cut and burn on his
body, and his muscles ached with
tiredness. But worse was the despair,
knowing Gore now had the Shadow

Sword back after a thousand years.

I've handed Gore his most powerful weapon. I should never have brought it here!

Shadows spiralled out from the blade, wrapping themselves around Gore. Jack's heart pounded as the General began to grow — taller and taller, wider and wider, until he was three times his original size. The Shadow Sword grew too, becoming the length of a helicopter blade.

"Now you will see true power!" shouted Gore, his voice shaking the ground like an earthquake.

He pointed the blade at the smoke

billowing above his head. It thickened into a dark blanket, blocking out the light from the crystals. Then he pointed the blade at the shadows between the rocks. They bulged and twisted, forming hunched hyenas with dagger-like teeth. With terrible roars, they leapt at Jack. He reached for his sword out of habit — but of course, the scabbard was empty.

He stumbled back, raising his hands over his face. He braced himself, expecting at any moment to feel teeth sink into him ... But in a flash of light, the shadow hyenas disappeared.

"Ruby!" cried Jack. She was running

over, her eyes still glowing from the fire-beam she'd shot at the hyenas. Danny was beside her. He swung his club at another creature, knocking it aside. Hope spread through Jack. *While the three of us fight together, we've got a chance!*

Gore was still using the sword to create packs of shadow hyenas. They sprinted towards Jack and his friends, howling.

This time Jack didn't take a step back. He charged straight at them. Ducking a swiping paw, he grabbed the first hyena by the neck. He swung it in a low arc, throwing it crashing

into three others. A second hyena
slashed him across the arm but he
ignored the pain and punched it
with all his strength. It sailed away
through the air. Ruby's eyes flashed
and sizzled as she blasted a group of
the creatures. Danny grunted as he

swung his club, keeping more of the enemies at bay. When Smarm and Bulk came close, Ruby turned her fiery eyes on them, forcing them back.

Nonetheless, there were so many shadow hyenas that Jack, Ruby and Danny were surrounded. The creatures padded in a tight circle around Jack and his friends, waiting for the moment to finish their prey.

"Maybe coming to rescue me wasn't such a great idea after all," Danny said, panting.

"We're not finished yet," Jack said.

The hyenas pounced. Jack heard the hiss of Ruby's eyes, and Danny's grunts as he swung his club. Jack aimed his fists at a tide of claws and snarling teeth. He felt a powerful blow from behind and went down hard on the rocky ground. Slavering hyenas swarmed over him, pinning him down.

"Jack!" Ruby cried. He caught a glimpse of her terrified face before he was swamped by writhing shadows.

"Goodbye, Chosen One," Gore cried in triumph.

Jack felt a sharp pain as teeth sank into his leg.

It's all over.

But suddenly the pack of hyenas whined and scattered. Jack blinked in astonishment to see the air beside him shimmering. A figure appeared out of nowhere. His heart surged as he recognised her purple hair.

"Thank goodness I've found you," Ms Steel said, helping Jack up. "I tracked your Oracles." She paused to kick a hyena that had come too close, sending it hissing in retreat. "Take this," she said, thrusting a long package wrapped in cloth into Jack's hand. Jack unwrapped it to reveal ...

"Another sword?" he said. The finish of the blade was dull and mottled grey. Jack felt the edge with his finger and was surprised how blunt it felt.

"Not just any sword," Ms Steel replied quickly. "Its name is Blaze and it's made of sunsteel. You'll see its power when—"

But she was cut off by the sizzling crackle of a blaster shot. Ms Steel cried in pain and slumped forward into Jack's arms.

"No!" Jack cried. He looked over her shoulder to see the smirking Smarm creep out from behind a rock, a blaster in his hands.

"I'll be OK, Jack," Ms Steel whispered. "Trust in your powers — and trust the sword. It will know you're the one holding it ..." She shimmered again and was gone.

The pack of hyenas circled around
them once more, barking and howling.
Danny swung his club, trying to hold
them back. Ruby was directing a
constant stream of fire at them.

Jack felt a heavy wave of dread as
General Gore strode towards him,
eyes flashing with fury. The General
towered over Jack. He raised the
Shadow Sword, its blade twice as
long as Jack's body. Surely this new
weapon was no match for it.

Gore brought the Shadow Sword
slicing down. Jack threw up the
new sword in a desperate parry. It

clashed with the Shadow Sword with a piercing ring. To Jack's surprise, he hardly felt the impact as the blade soaked up the force of the blow.

This sword is stronger than it looks.

"Your defence is sound," the General said. "Rex has trained you well. But let's see how you fight when you're distracted."

The General took a step back and pointed over Jack's shoulder at Danny and Ruby. They were crawling away from five shadow hyenas. The glow of Ruby's eyes had died and there was a cut along her cheek. Two of the hyenas leapt at her, yanking the mirror shield from her grip. Danny had lost his club and was trying to kick the dogs away.

I have to save them!

Jack knew that turning his back on the General would leave him open to attack. But he couldn't leave his friends to be torn apart.

The Shadow Sword sang once more through the Noxxian air, cleaving towards Jack. He spun away from it and towards his friends, holding the dull grey blade above his head in the hope it would protect him. With a piercing shriek, the swords clashed once more and Jack was thrown forward. Scrambling to his feet, Jack saw that Gore was staring at him, holding a hand over his face. His robes were lit up with a golden glow. Jack looked down at his sword, and saw, with amazement, a pure yellow light shining from it, like the midday sun. He felt power vibrate through his arm and remembered what Ms Steel had called the weapon: Blaze.

She's given me the chance to win!

CHAPTER 6

ESCAPE FROM NOXX

THE LIGHT grew brighter and
brighter until Jack couldn't bear to
look at it any more. He felt himself
infused with a new energy, a new
hope. The light swept across the rocky
terrain like a dazzling sunrise. The
shadow hyenas howled and turned
away. Bulk cried out, shielding his

eyes. Smarm threw his long cloak around himself. Danny and Ruby shook off the cowering hyenas and rose to their feet, grabbing their weapons.

Jack swung the sword at the closest hyena and it disappeared in a flash of light, leaving only an echoing howl. Cutting and sweeping, Jack advanced on the pack. One touch of the blade destroyed the hyenas.

"The weapon of Solus!" Gore cried, backing away. There was a note of fear in his voice.

Solus? thought Jack. But there was no time to wonder what that might be. He advanced and sliced at the General, the blade catching his leg and cutting through the black armour. The General hissed in pain and Jack gritted his teeth with satisfaction as Gore shrank back down to his normal size.

"No! You shall not defeat me!" Gore screamed with fury and slashed the Shadow Sword at Jack.

Drawing on all his super-strength, Jack swung Blaze to meet the blow.

The swords smashed together with a blast of energy that threw Jack back across the rocky ground. He looked up to see the General standing still, staring in shock at his hand. It held just a hilt with a jagged piece of blade still attached — all that was left of the Shadow Sword.

Danny and Ruby were staring too, open-mouthed. Smarm gave a shriek of horror.

Great gouts of shadow streamed from the broken Shadow Sword, spiralling upwards with a rustling, crackling hiss. Gore held it out in front of him.

"This isn't over," he told Jack, his red eyes blazing. "You will never defeat me!"

"I will," Jack told him, jaw clenched.

"Remember the prophecy? *Darkness will rise and conquer light, unless the Chosen One joins the fight.* I'm the Chosen One, Gore — and I'm going to

defeat you now!"

Jack whipped Blaze in a sideways slash, knocking the broken remains of the Shadow Sword out of Gore's hands. Gore gave a terrible cry. Losing the sword seemed to drain him of his powers and he slumped to his knees.

It's over!

"You did it, Jack!" Ruby cried, rushing over to him.

"Nice work, buddy," Danny said, clapping him on the back.

A tremble shook the ground. From where he was slumped, General Gore looked up at Jack. He opened his mouth to reveal blackened, crooked

100

teeth. A strange sound spluttered from his throat. It took a second for Jack to realise it was laughter.

"You think you've won," the General said. "But you have merely sealed your own doom."

The ground shook again, more heavily. Rocks began to fall from the ceiling. Jack watched in horror as one of the stalactites snapped, crashing to the ground in an explosion of rock and debris.

"We have to get out of here," Ruby cried in terror.

General Gore was already on his feet. "This isn't over, Chosen One," he shouted, and ran towards the palace.

But the palace was shaking. Its balcony buckled and collapsed. As Gore reached the doors, there was a huge *BOOM*. The twisted towers sheared off and slid down, followed by the roof and walls. A great avalanche of rubble came rushing down on to the General. He raised his arms and gave a bellow of rage, before the stones buried him completely.

"No, Master!" Smarm wailed. He and Bulk ran over to the collapsed palace.

Great cracks ran across the cavern ceiling. Rocks crashed down all around them and the air was

thick with dust. Smarm picked up
something from the rubble and
clutched it to himself. It was Gore's
broken helmet.

"Let's go," said Jack, "before we're
buried too."

"But how can we get out of here?" Ruby asked, sidestepping a falling boulder. "We haven't got the Portal Orb, remember?"

"No," Jack said, as a thought occurred to him. "But the orb isn't the only machine that can create a portal. Follow me!"

He ran back towards the stalactite where Danny had been imprisoned by Skulgar, his friends close behind. By a huge crater was the row of black jet-like vehicles.

"Of course," Ruby said. "The Portal Ships! We can ride one ... Can't we?"

"We have to try." Jack peered

into the closest ship. Rows of seats, which had obviously been meant for Noxxian warriors, lined the cabin. Jack climbed through the cockpit door, and Ruby and Danny followed. Jack took a seat at the controls. He flinched as a piece of rock landed on the dark-tinted glass of the screen in front of him. Lights blinked on the console, and there was a joystick.

"Hawk, what do I do?" Jack said.

"First you'll need to set our course for Hero Academy. That's forty-one degrees north, nineteen degrees west."

Jack punched the numbers into the screen.

"Use the joystick to accelerate and steer. Press the purple button on your right to launch."

Jack took a deep breath. Knowing how the controls worked was one thing, being able to fly a Noxxian craft through a collapsing cavern was something else. *Let's hope those hours spent playing on my games console will finally pay off.*

He pressed the launch button. "Hang on to your seats!" The engines roared and Jack slammed the thruster fully forward. The ship shot into the air. Ruby cried out as she tumbled off her chair.

"You forgot to tell them to fasten their seatbelts," Hawk said, as Jack eased the joystick back and forth, carefully weaving the craft in and out of falling rocks.

Jack buckled up with one hand, hearing the others do the same behind him.

"Would you like me to take you through the rest of the safety procedures?" Hawk asked cheerfully.

"Just tell me how to open the portal," Jack said, trying to concentrate.

"Oh, that's easy," Hawk said as a shower of stones rattled against the windscreen. *"There's a big red lever right in front of you—"*

But before Hawk could finish, Jack saw the entire ceiling give way with a massive, grinding roar and come rushing down at them. There was nowhere to go, no escape. Jack heard

Danny gasp.

"No!" Ruby cried.

Jack pulled the lever.

A wall of shadow appeared before them, swirling and boiling. The Portal Ship plunged into it ...

And emerged into bright light.

Jack blinked and peered ahead through the cracked, dusty glass, seeing a row of trees racing towards them.

"Watch out!" Danny shouted, but it was too late.

Jack shielded his face as the ship slammed into the trunks at a terrific speed and smashed right through with a tortured scream of tearing metal. Jack felt himself thrown forward hard against the seatbelt, then back as they dropped sharply. He slowed the vessel and aimed for a landing on a bank of grass. Jack was flung forward again as they hit the ground. The Portal Ship groaned and skidded before coming to a stop in a bank of mud.

"Is everyone OK?" Jack called out.

"Sort of," Danny said. Light flooded the ship as the hatch was torn open. Two silver-suited kids with red shoulder patches pointed energy weapons in at them. Behind them,

Jack grinned as he saw Chancellor Rex peering into the shuttle in amazement.

We made it back!

"I may be able to see into the future," the Chancellor said, "but this is one thing I certainly didn't predict."

Jack unstrapped himself and half-fell out of the Portal Ship into the bright sunlight of the school grounds. A great rush of students ran round Jack, Ruby and Danny, all clapping them on the backs and cheering.

"You did it," a girl from Blue House shouted. "All the other Noxxian portals have closed! You saved the world!"

Jack saw Professor Rufus stare, amazed, at the Noxxian vessel, then at Jack and his friends. "How ...?" he began, before trailing off.

Other teachers were gathered, the visors of their Oracles lowered, and weapons in their hands. Jack couldn't

see Ms Steel among them.

She must be resting after
teleporting back from Noxx.

"I think a celebration is in order!"
Chancellor Rex said, his face
wrinkling into a wide smile.

"I could kill for a burger," said

Danny, grinning. "You don't want to know what Noxxian food is like. OK, maybe you do. Slugs, mostly."

Jack, Danny and Ruby were hoisted on to the shoulders of their fellow students and carried in honour across the courtyard. Jack saw Olly and his gang lurking away from the crush of students. Jack gave him a wave and grinned when Olly nodded back grudgingly.

"Even Olly thinks you're a hero, Jack," Ruby said, laughing.

They were set down outside the dining hall, where long tables were being hurriedly prepared for the feast to be held in their honour.

Jack had defeated Gore and stopped the Noxxian invasion. Not bad for the boy who used to be nicknamed Beak the Freak.

Except I'm not Beak the Freak any more. I'm Jack Beacon, the Chosen One, and a student at Hero Academy.

"I'm very proud of you, Jack," Chancellor Rex said, patting him on the shoulder as he took his seat. "I look forward to seeing what else you accomplish here at Hero Academy."

"But Noxx is gone, isn't it?" Jack asked. "Isn't the world safe now?"

"The Noxxians are scattered, but

not gone. And there are other enemies besides General Gore who want to see our world fall to darkness. Shadows rise, Jack, but, remember, so does the sun." The Chancellor winked at him.

With his friends by his sides, there was nothing Jack couldn't do. Whatever threats the world might face, Jack and Team Hero were there to protect it.

THE END

VENTURA WAS A VILLAGE THEN, ON THE
SITE WHERE VENTURA CITY STANDS
TODAY. GRETCHEN GATHERED A GROUP OF
WARRIORS TO TAKE ON GENERAL GORE
AND HIS FORCES. ONE WARRIOR WAS
FROM THE DESERT REALM OF SOLUS,
ANOTHER FROM THE UNDERWAT...
SEQUANA, AND MANY ...
AROUND THE W...
HAD SP...

they soon wo
...ntura, a you...
...the power of
...the site where
...d a group
...rces. One
...other from
...d other
...owers,
...a secret
...ese

TIMETABLE

	MON	TUE	WED	THUR	FRI
	ASSEMBLY	ASSEMBLY	ASSEMBLY	ASSEMBLY	ASSEMBLY
	POWERS	POWERS	POWERS	POWERS	POWERS
	COMBAT	STRATEGY	TECH	COMBAT	STRATEGY
	MATHS	GEOGRAPHY	ENGLISH	HISTORY	ENGLISH
	HISTORY	SCIENCE	MATHS	SCIENCE	GEOGRAPHY
	LUNCH!				
13.00				STRATEGY	WEAPON TRAINING
14.00	TECH	COMBAT	COMBAT	GYM	GYM
15.00	GYM	GYM	WEAPON TRAINING	GYM	HOMEWORK
16.00	GYM	GYM	GYM	GYM	FREE
	HOMEWORK	HOMEWORK	HOMEWORK	HOMEWORK	

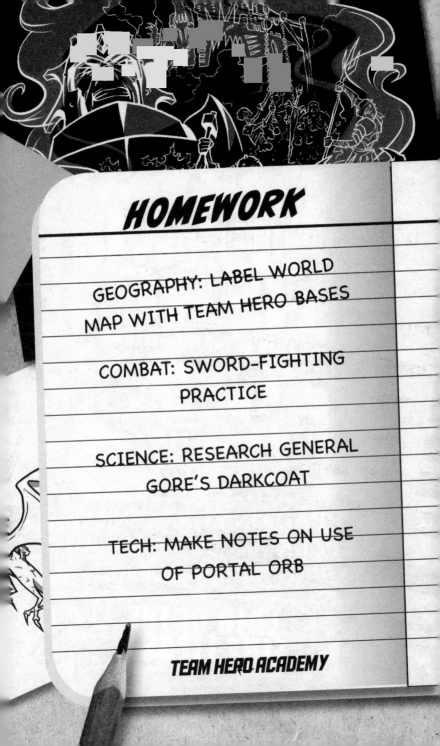

HOMEWORK

GEOGRAPHY: LABEL WORLD
MAP WITH TEAM HERO BASES

COMBAT: SWORD-FIGHTING
PRACTICE

SCIENCE: RESEARCH GENERAL
GORE'S DARKCOAT

TECH: MAKE NOTES ON USE
OF PORTAL ORB

TEAM HERO ACADEMY

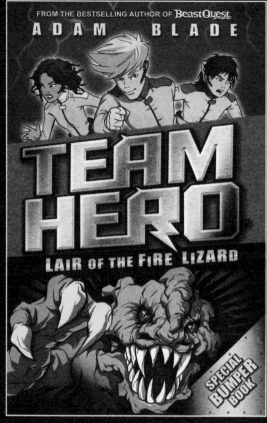

READ ON FOR A SNEAK
PEEK AT THIS SPECIAL
BUMPER BOOK:

LAIR OF THE
FIRE LIZARD

CHAPTER 1

A MISSING FRIEND

JACK JUMPED back as a geyser spurted from the ground only ten metres from where he was walking. The jet of steaming water arced into the air then cascaded down, splashing the trousers of Jack's silver snowsuit.

"This place is amazing!" said Ruby, her amber eyes shining.

"As long as you don't get boiled alive," said Jack, eyeing the bare rocky ground.

"I'll listen out for anything else that

might cook us," said Danny, tucking his straight black hair behind his bat-like ears.

All around them, among the stunted trees and boulders, pools of turquoise water glistened. The strangest thing was how icy the air was, even though they were practically walking on a volcano. But then, they *were* in the Arctic Circle.

"Hawk, switch to infrared vision," Jack said.

"Wonderful idea!" replied the Oracle in his ear. *"The landscape will be even more impressive in thermal vision."*

A visor extended from the earpiece

over Jack's eyes. The terrain showed in shades of blue and white, with hotspots of orange, yellow and red.

If only we were here just to enjoy the view.

But they were on a Team Hero mission.

Check out the Special Bumper Book: LAIR OF THE FIRE LIZARD to find out what happens next!

WIN AN ADVENTURE PARTY AT GO APE TREE TOP JUNIOR*

WITH

How would you like to win an epic party at Go Ape! for you and five of your friends?

You'll get up to an hour of climbing, canopy exploring, trail blazing and obstacles and a certificate to take away too!

The Go Ape! leafy hangouts are the perfect place to get together for loads of fun and prove that you've got what it takes to be the ultimate hero.

For your chance to win, just go to

TEAMHEROBOOKS.CO.UK

and tell us the names of the evil creatures that feature in the four different Team Hero books.

Closing date 31st October 2017

PLEASE SEE the website above for full terms and conditions.
*SUITABLE FOR 4 - 12 years old, but open to any age child over 1m tall.

IN EVERY BOOK OF
TEAM HERO SERIES
ONE there is a special
Power Token. Collect
all four tokens to get
an exclusive Team Hero
Club pack. The pack
contains everything you and
your friends need to form your
very own Team Hero Club.

MEMBERSHIP CARDS · MEMBERSHIP CERTIFICATE · STICKERS · POWER GAME · BOOKMARKS

Just fill in the form below, send it in with your four tokens
and we'll send you your Team Hero Club Pack.

SEND TO: Team Hero Club Pack Offer, Hachette Children's Books,
Marketing Department, Carmelite House, 50 Victoria Embankment,
London, EC4Y 0DZ.

CLOSING DATE: 31st December 2017

WWW.TEAMHEROBOOKS.CO.UK

FIND THIS SPECIAL
BUMPER BOOK ON SHELVES
FROM OCTOBER 2017